Toucan!

D0238526

First published in Great Britain 2005
by Egmont Books Ltd
239 Kensington High Street, London W8 6SA
Text copyright © Sue Mayfield 2005
Illustrations copyright © Rochelle Padua 2005
The author and illustrator have asserted their moral rights.
Paperback ISBN 1 4052 1793 6
1 3 5 7 9 10 8 6 4 2
A CIP catalogue record for this title is available from the British Library.
Printed in U.A.E.

Too Tall

I Can't Fly

Big Yellow Beak

For

George

S.M.

For

Sharon (aka The Other Dodgy Person)
Wojciech
The Paduas
. . . and Ebony.

R.P.

Too Tall

Giraffe is very tall.

When Giraffe plays in the park with Penguin and Toucan he bangs his head on the swings.

'You're too tall!' says Penguin.

When Giraffe goes for tea at
Toucan's house he is too tall to
get in the door.

'You're too tall,' says Toucan.

When Giraffe goes to the cinema
nobody can see past his head!
'You're too tall!' say the people
behind him.

Giraffe is sad. 'I'm too tall,' he says.

Then one day Penguin flies her kite.

The wind is very strong. It blows

Penguin's kite up into a tree.

Penguin can't reach her kite. She
tries to jump but she is too small.

She tries to climb

but she falls down.

'Help!' says Penguin.

15

Toucan tries to fly up to the tree.

But the wind is too strong.

He can't fly high enough.

'Help!' says Toucan.

'I can do it!' says Giraffe.

Giraffe stretches up tall

into the tree.

He can reach

Penguin's kite easily.

He brings it down again.

'Thank you, Giraffe,' says Penguin.

'I'm glad you're so tall!'

'Hoorah for Giraffe!' says Toucan.

I Can't Fly

Toucan likes to fly. He flies up in the sky. He flies higher than Giraffe's head.

'Look at me!' says Toucan.

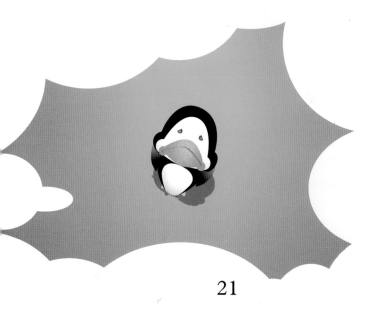

Penguin wants to fly too. 'I wish

I could fly like Toucan,' she says.

Penguin tries to fly.

She stands on a chair and jumps off.

Bump!

Penguin lands with a
crash.

Ow!

'I can't fly,' she says sadly.

'Try again,' says Toucan.

So Penguin tries running fast.

'Faster! Faster!' says Giraffe.

But Penguin still can't fly.

Penguin tries flapping her wings.

'Flap them harder,' says Toucan.

But Penguin's wings aren't big

enough. She still can't fly.

Penguin is sad. So the friends play

football to cheer her up.

But Giraffe

kicks

the ball too hard . . .

. . . and it lands in the river.

'Oops!' says Toucan.

'Help!' says Giraffe. 'I can't swim.'

'I can swim!' says Penguin. She

jumps into the water.

Penguin can swim very fast. She can even swim underwater like a fish. In no time at all she brings the football back to Giraffe and Toucan.

'Hoorah!' they say. 'We're glad you

can swim, Penguin!'

Big Yellow Beak

Toucan's beak is big and yellow.

Bright yellow.

Banana beak!

Other birds laugh at Toucan's beak. 'Banana beak!' they call him.

It's so bright!

'Don't listen to them,' says Penguin.

But Toucan is sad.

'I wish my beak was grey or black like other birds,' he says.

I like your beak!

'Come for a walk with us, Toucan,' says Giraffe. But Toucan doesn't want to. 'People will see me and laugh,' he says.

So Giraffe and Penguin go
for a walk without Toucan.
Giraffe and Penguin walk
a long way.

They walk so far that they get lost.

It starts to get dark.

Penguin and Giraffe are frightened.

'Help!' they say.

Giraffe and Penguin
have been gone a long
time. Toucan is worried.

43

So he goes to look for them. He flies

a long way through the dark night.

Suddenly, Giraffe spots Toucan's
bright yellow beak.

Toucan!

'Look!' he says. 'It's Toucan!'

Toucan's beak is very bright. His friends can see it even in the dark! Toucan flies in front of Giraffe and Penguin.

'Follow my beak!' says Toucan.

'I can lead you home.'

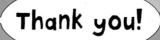

Thank you!

'Thank you, Toucan,' says Penguin.

'Hoorah for Toucan's big yellow

beak!' says Giraffe.